LOOSE GEMS

STORIES ABOUT LIFE, LOVE & BUSINESS

Loose Gems

Stories About Life, Love & Business

Sidney Thal

DEDICATION

To Berta

My Life

My Love

My Partner

CREDITS

Edited by Walt Crowley
Designed by Marie McCaffrey
Produced by Crowley Associates, Inc.
Cover portrait by Sydney R. Cohen
Copyright 1998, Sidney Thal.

Address Inquiries to:
Fox's Gem Shop
1341 Fifth Avenue
Seattle, Washington 98101
(206) 623-2528

ISBN 0-9664745-0-3
First Printing, June 1998

C O N T E N T S

When creating a piece of jewelry, designers examine loose gems to find the ones perfect for the concept they have in mind. Gems are stored in folded papers to keep them safe and separated. It's only when they're pulled out and put in the light that their many facets shine. And it's only when the diamonds rest near the emeralds and rubies, sapphires and amethysts that their rainbow varieties reveal their unique properties.

Sidney's gems, loosely collected in this book, give testimony to a life well lived, not just a living well made. He is a good man, a husband for sixty-two years, father of three children, grandfather of four, and greatgrandfather of one, so far. He keeps in touch with his many nephews and nieces, real and honorary, and has hundreds of friends whose ages range from ninety-eight years to two.

At eighty-eight, his days are full. He still golfs, writes, visits Fox's everyday when he's in Seattle, and has a busy social life. He keeps abreast of the world's happenings and his neighbors'. He continues to learn, to grow, to create.

When we are born, we are like a smooth piece of cotton. As our life progresses, the fabric of our existence becomes detailed in pattern, thick in texture, nubby with lost and added stitches. My dad's life, a long and blessed one, has become like a fine tapestry whose threads, burnished by experience, shine like jewels.

Cynthia Muscatel

January 1998

Why My Son-in-Law Made Me Advertising Manager.
by Sid Thal

Everybody thought we were crazy when my wife Berta and I invested a fortune in a new jewelry store in 1986. Maybe we were. We were 70 and 60. We'd built a fine little gem shop and put away enough money to retire. But we were both active in the business and the community. We had no desire in selling out because family owned businesses were an endangered species. When we were offered 4000 square feet on the prime corner of Fifth & Union, we took it. My son-in-law, a very good school teacher, also a very talented artist, came into the business. The first thing he did was design a pair of diamond penny-loafer buttons.

Truth In Advertising

The truth is, I was more than a little perplexed. There wasn't a tremendous demand for 18 karat gold penny-loafer buttons. But when his design won an international contest, I was very proud! He worked hard, studied the industry, and turned out to be a darned good businessman. But I was skeptical.

The Generation Gap

You have to understand something. when I started in the jewelry business. my son-in-law wasn't born. When Berta and I bought Fox's in 1948, he was still wearing diapers. I guess I wanted my son-in-law to come up the long and hard way like Berta and I did. But obviously, we didn't have time. Two years after he started, he became manager. And four years after that, he was president. I am happy to tell you that despite the recession, national decline in retail sales, and proliferation of suburban stores. Fox's is doing better than ever before.

A Tough Hat To Fill

Now don't think my son-in-law is perfect. We don't agree on everything. But the common values we share transcend the differences. Harry Fox started Fox's in 1912. And he built his little jewelry store by offering his clients quality, value, honesty and integrity. Berta and I were determined to carry on that tradition. My son-in-law and daughter share that

philosophy and it works even better today than it did before. Because sadly, there isn't the kind of ethics today in business that there used to be. My son-in-law has made a lot of changes. Most of those who worked for me have retired. And over the years he has replaced them with truly exceptional people. They are all well trained jewelry professionals who can give you the kind of service you can't get anywhere else. He's traveled to places I've never heard of and developed loyal relationships with talented designers and artists, so that today Fox's Gem Shop offers things you'll be surprised to find in Seattle. And that's not an advertising slogan. And who am I to argue with success?

The Only Bone I Have To Pick With My Son-In-Law Is The Advertising

"It's nowhere near as good as it was when I used to drive my cab up Fifth Avenue wearing my bowler," I argued. "I talk to people everyday," I said "and they ask me what I do for a living. I tell them I work for Fox's and they don't know what Fox's is. Just because we've been around for eighty-five years doesn't mean everybody knows us."

"OK," my son-in-law said, "I'm not going to argue with you anymore." And he appointed me advertising manager. My son-in-law is a smart man...he married my daughter. He said he'd try me out and gave me six months to prove myself. So please support me. Buy something at Fox's. At 88, I'm not likely to be able to get another job right away.

Sincerely

Sid Thal
Advertising and Chairman of the Board

FOX'S Fifth & Union

Seattle's Jeweler Since 1912

1341 FIFTH AVENUE SEATTLE, WA 98101 (206) 623-2528
Parking validated at Rainier Square Garage on Union between 5th and 4th
1-800-733-2528

INTRODUCTION

I n the spring of 1993, Sidney Thal's daughter Cyndy suggested that he take up writing. He had never written seriously before so, a few months shy of his 84th birthday, he joined the Palm Springs Writers Guild, and found he loved the art. Not long after, he began to pen little squibs of advertising copy for Fox's Gem Shop, which he and his wife Berta owned in Seattle.

Thus was launched Sid's latest career as a writer, but he already had lots of practice as an irrepressible storyteller — and his life afforded no shortage of material.

Sid's father, Samuel, fled the Russian occupation of the Baltic states at the turn of the century and settled in London, where he went to work as a tailor on Saville Row. His brothers had taken the same route earlier, but they pressed on to the United States and ultimately settled in Bellingham, Washington.

After a few years, Samuel also crossed the Atlantic and took up his trade in Boston. He married a Russian emigre, Gertrude — or Gitel, affectionately — and changed his name to Rosenthal because it sounded more dignified. Gitel gave birth to Sidney, the first of two sons, on July 15, 1909, in Malden, Massachusetts.

Radicalized by the Hyde Park orators he had heard in London and the deplorable exploitation of American garment workers, Samuel became a labor organizer. His zeal won the notice of the great socialist Eugene V. Debs — and less approving attention from the local constabulary.

One of Sid's earliest memories is the Sunday that his parents' flat was raided by the police. The pretext was that they were playing whist on the Sabbath in defiance of Boston's notorious Blue Laws. It was really a warning, and even Debs advised him to cool his ardor. After her husband was jailed several times, Gitel suggested it might be best to move the family west.

Samuel joined his four brothers in Bellingham in 1916, set up his own clothing shop, and eventually reclaimed his original family name. Although the family was far from affluent, Sid and his brother Sol grew up in a household rich with music, culture, love, and dreams of building a better, more just world.

Sid delivered newspapers to help the family finances, mastered tennis to become the city champion of Bellingham, practiced the piano and gave recitals accompanied by Sol on the violin. He attended the predecessor of Western Washington University. He met his future wife Berta while taking piano lessons and followed her to the University of Washington in Seattle. He took a job at the Weisfield and Goldberg's jewelry store near campus.

The stock market crash of 1929 sent the store into bankruptcy, ending both Sid's employment and his studies. He found what work he could find as a traveling salesman and crisscrossed the nation before settling down in Portland, where Berta's brother owned a coat factory. The couple married in 1934 and went on the road together as a sales team. Unfortunately, the coats didn't fit, so they took up marketing a new hair rinse, which also didn't perform as advertised.

Berta became pregnant with their first child, Stephen, in 1940. The couple returned to Bellingham and moved in with Berta's parents. Leo Weisfield was back in business and gave Sid a job in his credit department.

Following Pearl Harbor, Sid took a civilian post supervising the loading and unloading of Navy ships at Seattle's giant Piers 90-91. With the end of the war and a second child, Cynthia, to feed, he went to work managing the downtown Seattle gem shop founded by Harry Fox back in 1912, and later owned by Herb Meltzer.

When Meltzer decided to sell the tiny business in the Skinner Building, Berta and Sid scraped together $15,000 in cash and borrowed more from family and friends. On February 9, 1948, they became the proud but impoverished owners of a sparsely stocked gem shop. They kept the name "Fox's" because they couldn't afford to repaint the sign on the door. Fox's survived the early struggles and the store was on a solid footing by 1950 when the Thals' youngest child, Joy, arrived.

Sid and Berta Thal's public personae were forged by a

happy accident in 1966, when they joined several other couples in buying a classic London taxi at that year's Poncho art auction. The other buyers soon lost interest in the 1954 Austin cab, and Sid and Berta became the vehicle's sole owners.

Sid became a familiar sight as he toured the town in his shiny black taxi, and he completed the image with a bowler hat acquired during a trip to London. Fox's advertising consultant, David Stern, recognized public relations gold when he saw it, and he transformed the dapper Anglophile and his statuesque wife into the personifications of Seattle elegance.

Completion of the new Rainier Tower in 1980 gave Sid and Berta the opportunity to escape their cramped store in the Skinner Building. Although entering their seventies, when most people had already retired, they took on the task of moving and expanding Fox's Gems.

A few years later, Berta and Sid found a willing helper in their new son-in-law, Chai Mann. An artist by training, Chai quickly demonstrated his talents for both jewelry design and marketing. He was soon running the store — with lots of advice from his father-in-law — and serving a new generation of clientele while preserving the traditions of service, quality, and integrity established by Berta and Sid.

Although Berta later fell into a long illness (she died in 1996), Sid was not ready to fade into the background. He leapt at David Stern's idea for a series of magazine and newspaper ads in which Sid could tell stories, philosophize, instruct, joke, and publicly needle his son-in-law. David initially acted as scribe, but Sid was soon writing on his own.

We have selected thirty of these advertisements from the scores that have appeared. They have been edited slightly and rearranged into three chapters, "The Business," "Dialogues with My Son-in-Law," and "Life and Love." Four examples of Sid Thal's more serious short fiction complete this volume.

This collection of *Loose Gems* has been assembled chiefly for your enjoyment, but if you decide to drop in at Fox's and perhaps buy a gem of the mineral variety, Sid won't be offended.

The Editor

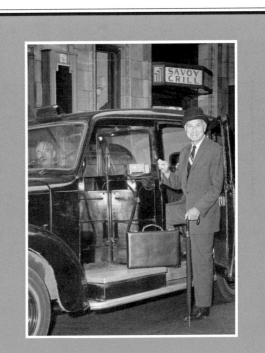

THE BUSINESS:

Matty Singer Made Us What We Are Today
"I've Probably Examined More Diamonds Than Dr.
Spock Has Examined Babies" • To TV or Not to TV
Economics 101 • Mr. Fox, Your Pants • The Pope's Ring
Money • Time Flies • "It's Too Expensive for You, But
I'll Show It to You Anyway."

Back in 1948 banks didn't make loans to people starting a new business. So when my wife Berta and I decided to buy Fox's Gem Shop, we scraped together $15,000 and borrowed the rest from our families.

Six weeks passed before we made our first major sale, for $5000. Instead of using the money to buy more jewelry to sell, we paid back the family. That left us short of merchandise, so Berta put out twelve Royal Dalton tea cups we had received as a wedding gift. We had no idea how to price them. Berta arbitrarily marked them at $27.95 apiece, and they were gone!

We scoured every antique shop in Vancouver and Victoria and filled Fox's Gem Shop with tea cups. They took up more space than rings and earrings and pendants and bracelets. At least the shelves were not bare.

One day a woman and her teenage son walked in, leaving a man waiting for them on the street outside. She was from New York, on her way to Alaska, and she purchased several cups and saucers. She left the store and after a few minutes the man came in.

"My wife says you and your wife are a nice couple," he began, "but you can't live on selling tea cups. I'm in the diamond estate business in New York, I'm going to send you some merchandise." Two months later a package arrived, insured and registered, with about $50,000 worth of beautiful gems and a note, "Don't pay until you get the money. Sincerely, Matty Singer."

So, truly, he made Fox's what it is today.

"I'VE PROBABLY EXAMINED MORE DIAMONDS THAN DR. SPOCK HAS EXAMINED BABIES"

W hen I started examining diamonds, Dr. Spock was just starting to examine diapers. That was in 1926. I was 17 and worked for Weisfield & Goldberg's in Bellingham.

Meanwhile, in New York, a master diamond cutter from Belgium named Lazare Kaplan was cutting diamonds a new way. He used a mathematical formula developed by a Belgian physicist in 1918 that gave diamonds far more brilliance, sparkle, and fire than they'd ever had before. He called it the Ideal Cut Lazare Diamond. Even now, less than 1 percent of all diamonds in the world are ideal cut. Most diamond cutters don't choose his method because it uses more diamond material, and they are not thinking of quality or brilliance, just size. It also takes exacting skill.

In 1936, Lazare Kaplan was asked to cleave the second largest diamond ever found, the "Jonker." This 726 carat gem (one half pound!) was so valuable that Lloyds of London would not insure the cleavage. Lazare studied the stone for a year and the night before he was to make the cut, he had a dream that his plan was flawed and would shatter the stone. The next morning, he inked a new path and with one tap parted the gem. It was a perfect strike.

I bought diamonds directly from Lazare Kaplan until he died at age 107. Fox's continues to buy Lazare ideal cut diamonds from the company he founded. The Lazare Kaplan Co. achieved another milestone, a patented method of inscribing the girdle of a diamond with a laser. Now a diamond can be personalized and identified with a certified number or even have a special message or initials, just like a message of love you might inscribe on the back of a watch, lovely pin, or pendant.

I hope that someday you will have the pleasure of buying a fine diamond. I hope it will be an ideal cut diamond by Lazare Kaplan. And that you'll buy it from Fox's Gem Shop so we can send your message of love with it. A diamond is forever, you know.

TO TV OR NOT TO TV

My son-in-law hates television. "TV is full of killing, murder, fires, and everything horrible going on around us," he says. "I want us to be associated with happy events, like birthdays, marriages, and anniversaries."

Anyway, that is one of the reasons he gives me for not wanting to use TV in our advertising campaign. Fox's was the first fine jeweler in the United States to use radio in the early 50's, and we used TV a few years later. You might remember my old London taxi making its way to Fox's at Fifth and Union. It has been ten years since we stopped the ad and people talk as if they saw it just yesterday. This is the good side of advertising.

I let my son-in-law go on for a few minutes, so he could get it all out of his system. This was not the first time we have discussed his lack of desire to spend money on TV, and I am sure it won't be the last.

TV is not the only media with a negative slant, you

find it on the radio and in print as well. There are good people doing wonderful deeds every day, every minute out in the world, but who wants to write about them? You literally have to kill someone to make the news nowadays, but good people are still out there.

When Berta and I bought Fox's in 1948 most of our friends and competitors gave us six months before we would go broke. Nobody had to tell us what we had to do to be successful. We knew it would be an uphill battle. We had to give value and super service, make friends as well as customers. That is what Berta and I practiced, and we made it a tradition that today's staff still honors.

Twenty years later, when Nordstrom's stores were just starting their expansion, the late Lloyd Nordstrom got in touch with me and wanted Fox's to be part of their operation. They were going to open large stores in Tacoma, Portland, and Northern California. Although I had limited marketing and managerial skills, I thought we could do it and committed to their opening in Tacoma. After two months, I had my doubts. We had no staff to take over management of a new store. I was worried and losing sleep, so I called Lloyd, sat down with his brothers and staff and told my story.

"Forget it, Sid," he counseled. "I don't want you to worry or become sick over this. We'll manage somehow." I knew they had incurred heavy expenses building space tailored to our specifications. I had my check book with me, and I was about to write them a check.

"Don't fret, we will bill you. Take it easy," Lloyd told me as I left his office. You know, they never did send me a statement.

Like I said, there are good people out there. Lots of them. They just don't make headlines.

ECONOMICS 101

When my wife and I made our son-in-law president of Fox's, I decided to give him a degree in business. "There are two things that can really hurt you," I expounded in scholarly tones. "One is greed. Two is falling in love with the merchandise."

"Greed," I continued, "is so dangerous it can ruin your life as well as your business. And 'falling in love with the merchandise' should be the theme song of those marching into bankruptcy court." I knew the latter first hand.

In the early 1900's, my father had been a tailor in London's Saville Row. Years later he owned a small men's shop in Bellingham. What was hot back then (and now) was the new line of Levi Strauss pants. What was not hot was Papa's large inventory of herringbone wool trousers, which reminded him of the fine fabrics he had worked with in London.

"Get rid of the wool pants at cost and use the money to buy Levis," I pleaded, to no avail. Papa was in love with the merchandise.

When Berta and I bought Fox's in 1948, a delightful couple had a gallery next door to our original store in the Skinner Building. Their collection included lovely paintings by contemporary artists. The front window displayed their prize possession, a painting of a beautiful lady sitting by a stream.

One of our customers admired the canvas and finally went in to see if he could persuade the owners to sell the painting, but by then they had taken it home and it was no longer for sale. The gallery didn't survive the year.

Everything we have at Fox's is for sale. A few year's ago, we even sold my personal collection of Chinese furniture, netsukes, snuff bottles, and rare specimens.

We love our merchandise, but it's reserved for the customers.

MR. FOX, YOUR PANTS

My son-in-law sure knows how to keep me busy. "Do an ad on estate jewelry," he whispers as if it's a secret. "We have the most beautiful collection in town and you must have some great stories about antique jewelry." I have a humdinger that I'll get to in a minute.

There really is a big difference between estate jewelry, antique jewelry and new jewelry made up in old designs.

To be deemed "antique," you must be over 100 years old (so I'm safe for a few more years). It is very rare to find jewelry of such age in wearable condition. "Estate jewelry" is any previously owned jewelry. It may be from the early 1900's, but it may also be very current. Fox's specializes in pieces at least 40 years old. Period pieces are also very special because they are fine examples of the designs popular during a particular era.

What we pride ourselves on is genuine antique and estate jewelry. Remember, Fox's is always looking for older jewelry in good condition, and there is no charge to bring it in so that our expert jewelers can give you an idea of its value. Fox's also carries replicas of antique jewelry, made for us in England of 15 carat gold, carefully and beautifully mounted with quality gems. They are a great value, and will last a lifetime.

All of which reminds me of a trip I took to London some thirty years ago. When our son Steve, a certified gemologist, returned from serving with the U.S. Army in Korea, he went to work at Asprey's, London's exclusive jeweler to the Royal Family. One day he saw a notice that the Duke of Glouchester's collection of jewelry was being auctioned off at Christie's. He phoned, asking me to fly over to see it.

I came and we examined the lot, seeing many items we could use to great advantage in our stickpin bracelets. Altogether we came up with a price of 11,000 pounds, about 15,000 dollars at the time. Our bid was accepted.

The next day, one of London's infamous tabloids came out with the headline, "Yank Buys the Royal Jewelry for 11 Million Dollars [!!!], Plans to Take it to the U.S." Notwithstanding the faulty arithmetic, Eddie Gilmore of the Associated Press met us at the Savoy Hotel. His interview and photo of Steve and me went out on the AP wires and was picked up all across the U.S., winding up on the front page of *The Seattle Times* in November.

When I deplaned at Seatac, I was astonished to find myself a celebrity! The mayor wasn't there to greet me but a little customs officer with a big gold badge grabbed me by the arm and said with a big smile, "This way Mr.

Fox. I have a special place in line for you to get you out of here in a hurry."

It certainly was special. Two big agents went through my luggage like Sherman through Atlanta, piece by piece. I told them I had nothing to declare, not even a present for Berta or the children, but they were not convinced.

"Please come into my office," the little customs man with big gold badge finally said. In the office were the two big ex-football player types with little gold badges. One took my bowler hat and examined it minutely. The other broke the handle off of my umbrella and opened it. The little one went through my jacket, my wallet, felt in my shoes and drilled holes into the heels, and finally said "Please take off your pants, Mr. Fox." He did everything short of asking me to bend over. They gave my pants and shoes back, but not my umbrella.

I never did figure out what they were looking for, and they never told me.

The Pope's Ring

P ope John Paul II visited Brazil in 1980. He toured one barrio that was so poor and destitute that he removed his gold papal ring and gave it to be melted down to buy food for the needy.

A few months later, Seattle restaurateurs Mick McHugh and Tim Firnstahl took up a local collection to replace the Pope's ring and make a substantial donation to the Church. They asked us at Fox's to create a new ring in 18 carat gold with the papal insignia.

When it was finished, Mick and Tim organized a pilgrimage to the Vatican to present the ring to His Holiness. The group was led by Auxiliary Bishop Nicholas Walsh and included restaurateur Victor Rosellini and his wife Marci, and other Catholic friends. They invited Berta and me to come along as well, although we are Jewish. Along with Mick's Presbyterian fiance, Tracy French, we made it a truly ecumenical expedition.

We arrived in Rome, had drinks at the Jesuit university, and attended an enormous public Mass at St. Peter's.

Bishop Walsh said it didn't look like we'd get a private audience with the Pope, but then a Vatican official realized that we were unique. While the Pope had received many representatives from other faiths, we were in fact the first group to include three religions.

We were ushered into a private room and lined up to meet the Pope. He entered a few minutes later, smiling broadly amid flashing camera bulbs and a whirl of ecclesiastical excitement. The Pope proceeded down the line and chatted with each of us in turn.

When he came to Berta, she opened the box containing the new ring and said nervously, "I hope it fits."

"What means fits? Is someone ill?" he asked. (He was teasing us, since he speaks English and many other languages fluently.)

"No, no, Your Holiness," an aide explained. "She wants you to try it on."

The Pope slid the ring on his index finger, beamed, and announced, "See, it fits, it fits!"

Then he took my hand and pointed to the large jade ring I've worn for decades.

"This will fit, too," he said.

Fortunately for me, he chuckled and said that he was only making a joke.

I explained to him that Berta and I were Jewish and that we prayed that he would do everything in his power to promote better understanding among all who believed in God. He nodded his head and blessed us.

That night, Bishop Walsh introduced us to several Cardinals. When we related the story of the Pope's ring and the audience, they were very amused. They also seemed to have the same taste in jewelry.

One of the Cardinals said, "He can have the gold ring, but we'll take that big green one."

I wasn't so sure *he* was joking, but I laughed anyway. Then I stuck my hand in my pocket and kept it there until I and my ring were safely out of Rome.

MONEY

"I t's not your money until you spend it," my friend Charlie said.

"Great line," I told him. "Is it original or did you hear it?"

"It's not original and I don't remember." In his late eighties, like I am, he suffers from a little short-term memory loss. Who doesn't, I wonder.

I called my friend Kelly who has a doctorate in economics. He knows all about money and how to spend it, and does. I asked if he had ever heard the expression.

"That's a good one." he answered. "Very profound. Sure you didn't make that up to sell jewels to your customers at Fox's?"

That would be stooping too low, wouldn't it?

It was Ben Franklin who said, "A penny saved is a penny earned." Of course, he spent money like a drunken sailor when he was our ambassador to France. "Frugal Ben" and his purse were big hits with the ladies in Paris.

Speaking of frugal, we once had a customer whose wife for years brought back every Christmas present he gave her. "He works too hard for his money. He's a dentist and stands on his feet all day," she said, as she returned each beautifully wrapped package unopened.

"Better to have sore feet than a broken heart," I said to her one day in January, tired of hearing the same excuse year after year.

Too bad she couldn't see the love with which her husband selected every gift, the time he spent on his afternoon off just to find the right piece of jewelry for her.

At Fox's, we know about gifts. It doesn't have to take big money to make it a big moment for you and that special person.

And frankly, money can be such a pain. It needs attention, like a child. You worry about interest rates, inflation, the economy, and where and if to move it. Life is for living, so why not spread a little joy along the way.

Remember, "It's not your money until you spend it!"

P.S. This message is NOT sponsored by your local Savings & Loan.

P.P.S. The dentist still came in for many years for gifts. I often wondered for whom they were purchased, because they were never again returned.

Time Flies

My son-in-law is always coming up with new ideas. "We can't stand still," he says. "It's like time, it marches on and we must beat the drum and lead the parade."

I knew something else was coming, so I took a stance like George Washington crossing the Delaware. "Look who's talking about time. At 86, I feel like Father Time himself. I have the hardest time putting my socks on, and when I do, I can't get up."

George Burns said it even better: "When I finally find time to tie my shoes, I stay down there to see what else there is to do." If you think growing old is having the time of your life, it's time for you to think again.

Finally my son-in-law told me Fox's was going to have a big watch event.

Now, Fox's was never a watch store. We carried Rolex, Patek Philippe and Ebel, but there was always something about watches that made us unhappy. We were looking for the Holy Grail. Diamonds and magnificent colored gems, emeralds, rubies, and sapphires were our specialties.

I told my son-in-law, "I have been through this for fifty years. No more looking for the perfect watch. No to automatics, no to batteries, no. no, NO!"

So we had a watch event. Every major Swiss company sent a president or representative. The vendors said they had never seen so many fine watches under one roof. Ten vendors, five hundred customers. You're right, it was a big success and I ate crow again. I'm getting used to it.

More men are going back to fine Swiss mechanical, precision watches. There are hundreds of collectors in Seattle and across the United States who fit into Fox's mold. With two watch experts on staff, we have the time and patience to make your watch buying experience one you will remember.

Now for a few tips on your fine watch care. If your watch is mechanical and has to be wound, try to wind it at about the same time every day. Take the watch off when winding or changing the time, to avoid placing too much torque on the stem. If you can't wear it daily, wind it three or four times each week to keep the oil fluid. You will not save yourself a cleaning by letting it sit in a drawer, so keep it going.

If you are a good golfer or tennis player, never wear a mechanical watch while playing. Arm speeds of over seventy miles per hour can damage the movement. Finally, if you are the cook in the house, remember that water resistant does not mean steam-proof. Your watch is not a lobster, so don't steam it.

If you are still with me, thank you. My time is up.

> ## "IT'S TOO EXPENSIVE FOR YOU, BUT I'LL SHOW IT TO YOU ANYWAY."

Please excuse my sentimentality, but I've been thinking lately about a dear friend who taught me many valuable lessons. I've thought about writing a book about her but I'll settle for this ad for now.

Bernice Meggee was a liberated woman long before it was popular. In the Fifties, her husband was the distributor for RCA, Hotpoint and GE appliances in the West. When he passed away, everybody wanted to buy the franchise and the bank wanted Bernice to sell it. She decided to run it herself, and she did a great job.

One day Bernice walked into the Seattle branch of Hardy's, a prestigious New York jeweler, where Jay Jacobs is now. The manager recognized her and said "Good afternoon, Mrs. Meggee." When she asked to see the emerald ring in the window, he replied stuffily, "That's too expensive for you, but I'll show it to you anyway."

Bernice said thank you and walked up Fifth Avenue to Fox's.

"I'd like to see that ring," she said to my wife. Berta graciously pulled the emerald from the case and slipped it on Mrs. Meggee's finger. Voila! A sale and a sort of marriage were consummated.

Bernice Meggee became a lifelong friend and watched our children grow. She also helped Fox's grow to become one of America's fine jewelers, whereas Hardy's is long gone.

My son-in-law doesn't see where I am going with this ad. He thinks I'm just being nostalgic. He doesn't know that when he hires new employees, I take them aside one by one and tell the Bernice Meggee story. We have no place for arrogance at Fox's, I instruct. Never judge a book by its cover.

Above all, be kind and treat everyone right.

WHY MY SON-IN-LAW MADE ME ADVERTISING MANAGER

E verybody thought Berta and I were crazy in 1980 when we invested a fortune in a new jewelry store. Maybe we were.

We were pushing 70. We'd built a fine little gem shop and had put away enough money to retire. But we were both active in the business and in the community. We had no interest in selling out because family-owned businesses were an endangered species. So when we were offered 4,000 square feet on the prime corner of Fifth Avenue and Union Street, we took it.

My son-in-law Chai Mann was a school teacher at the time — a very good one — and a talented artist as well. He came into the business soon after the new store opened. The first thing he did was design a pair of gold and diamond buttons for penny loafers.

The truth is I was a little perplexed. There isn't a tremendous demand for 18 carat gold penny-loafer buttons.

Then his design won a national contest, and I was very proud. He worked hard, studied the industry, and turned out to be a darned good businessman. Despite this, I remained skeptical.

You have to understand something: When I started in the jewelry business, my son-in-law wasn't born. When Berta and I bought Fox's in 1948, he was still wearing diapers. I guess I wanted my son-in-law to come up the same long and hard way Berta and I had, but, obviously, he didn't have time.

Two years after he started, Chai became manager. Four years after that, he was president. He has weathered recessions, declines in downtown retail sales, and competition from suburban stores, and Fox's is doing better than ever before.

Now don't think my son-in-law is perfect. We don't agree on everything, but the common values we share transcend the differences. Harry Fox started his little jewelry store in 1912 and built it up by offering clients quality, value, honesty, and integrity. Berta and I were determined to carry on that tradition. My son-in-law and daughter share this philosophy, and Fox's has prospered in part because so few business uphold such high ethical standards.

My son-in-law has also made a lot of changes. Most of the people who used to work for Berta and me have retired, and over the years he has replaced them with a truly exceptional staff of well-trained jewelry professionals. He has traveled to places I've never heard of and developed loyal relationships with talented artists and designers, so that today Fox's Gem Shop offers things you literally can't find anywhere else. Who am I to argue with such success?

The only bone I have to pick with my son-in-law is the advertising.

"It's nowhere near as good as it was when I used to wear my bowler and drive up Fifth Avenue in my London Cab," I told him. "When I meet people and tell them I work at Fox's, they don't know what or where it is. Just because we've been around for eighty years doesn't mean everybody thinks of us."

"Okay," my son-in-law said. "I'm not going to argue with you." And he appointed me advertising manager on the spot.

My son-in-law is a smart man... he married my daughter. He said he'd try me out for six months. So please support me and buy something at Fox's. At 83, I'm not likely to find another job.

(This ad first appeared in April 1993. Mr. Thal was still employed as of this book's publication in April 1998.— Ed.)

NOT EXACTLY

"?"

My son-in-law asked me if I had finished the next ad, and when I said, "Not exactly," he laughed. He had just finished discussing a diamond purchased by a customer from another jewelry store, and I overheard the conversation.

My son-in-law asked the man the size of the diamond the man had purchased. "Was it one carat?"

The man replied, "Not exactly, it's about a carat."

My son-in-law asked whether the color was a "G" or an "H?"

"Not exactly, it's sort of off-white."

"How about clarity, imperfections, was it a VVS 1 or 2, or was it an SI 1 or 2?"

"Not exactly. It has a few flaws for identification purposes." By this time the anxious man was mopping his brow

"I hope I'm not making you feel uncomfortable with my questions?"

"Not exactly, but I hope there aren't many more."

"How about cut? Is it cut to ideal proportions to bring out its brilliance?" my son-in-law asked.

"Not exactly, it's cut to give maximum size, it's sort of spread, but it does have 58 facets!"

"Did you pay less than 5,000 dollars?"

"Not exactly."

"Can you get your money back?"

"Not exactly."

My son-in-law asked me if that's how the conversation really went.

"Not exactly," I said, "but close enough."

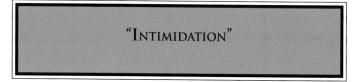

"Intimidation"

My son-in-law is upset with me because Fox's is such a beautiful store, and I wear a three-piece suit and a bowler hat. (I also shave every day and trim my moustache.)

"You intimidate the public," he starts out calmly. "A lot of people are afraid to come in. For years, your TV commercial showed you getting out of an old London taxi. I know it's a 1954 Austin but people think it's a Rolls! And then you look back at the camera through the glass door. Why didn't you at least leave the front door open and bow them in?!"

"I would have," I protested. "But it was colder than heck when we did that commercial."

Why is my son-in-law so upset these days? Being fifty must be getting to him. Wait until he hits his eighties!

I looked up "intimidate" in Webster's, and if he's right, I'm in trouble. "To make timid or fearful," it says in the dictionary. Is that Fox's? Is that the store Berta and I took over in the Skinner Building back in 1948?

I don't think so. If the store had a lot of class, well, we were a classy couple. Now in our mid-eighties, we still are.

But what has that got to do with people coming into Fox's? We've always had customers who come in wearing boots, jeans, tennis shorts, or sandals. Ninety percent of our staff dress city-casual. You can come in and find my son-in-law in tennis shoes or needing his beard trimmed. So what? He's a wonderful person and a great jeweler and designer.

You never have to worry about what you wear into our store, although we might have had a problem with the lady who ran past Fifth and Union wearing absolutely nothing. She didn't stop at Fox's (Darn it!) but she looked in at our neighbor, Eddie Bauer's. That was the most exciting thing to happen downtown in years. It even made Jean Godden's column in *The Seattle Times*.

I like to think Fox's offers something for everyone no matter what they're wearing (so long as they're wearing something), but I also know it's a new world out there. If you're not with it, you're out of it. I listen to my son-in-law and his staff. They are responsible for our continued success, and Berta and I are delighted.

I do want you to know, however, that I'm not changing the look of the store for anyone. But I might consider cutting back to a two-piece suit.

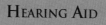

HEARING AID

"You know what?" my son-in-law said. "You should get a hearing aid."

"You know what?" I replied. "I don't need a hearing aid."

"Then why do you yell so loud when you are talking to your best friend, Fred Nielson?"

"Because Fred is 94 (same as Bob Hope), has a hearing aid, and doesn't use it," I barked back.

I have a friend who had the same trouble with his teeth. They are beautiful. They should be. He never wears them.

Well, that is the kind of dumb dialogue that my son-in-law and I get into when we find time to talk. He likes me to reminisce about old times, thinks it's an outlet for my frustrations.

It's true everything is changing, particularly with media and marketing. I remember the tiny little crystal set we had for a radio in 1925. With the TV, Internet and World Wide Web it's hard to know where to put your advertising dollars.

After five years of fighting with my son-in-law about TV advertising, he finally gave me a budget. Now that I have the money I don't know how to spend it!

"In the old days," my son-in-law says, "you had it easy. You had three or four TV stations. Now you have a hundred stations and a remote."

"What's that?" I asked. "Sorry, I didn't get it all."

(You think I need a hearing aid? I'll let you in on a secret — I have one.)

GREEN

My son-in-law rejected this ad three times. He said it had nothing to do with Fox's Gem Shop. "If you can tie it in," he said, "we'll run it, but not otherwise."

I came back with a beautiful ad with a smooth transition from green to jade, something we have in abundance at Fox's. My son-in-law didn't buy it.

"When you say green," I argued, "everybody thinks of jade." "Take a survey," he responded. So I asked my grandchildren what they thought of when I said "green." David, Jennifer and Zoey said "money." Zach said "spinach — yuck."

That triggered an idea. I tried tying green to money, like, "You don't have to spend much of it to get something very good at Fox's."

My wastebasket was filling up fast. I was out of ideas, but not memories.

Berta and I were married 62 years ago during the Great Depression. She was a teacher with five diplomas but no position. Then Weisfield and Goldberg's Jewelers went into receivership and I lost my job.

Those were very hard times, so when I was offered a job selling a new hair rinse called "Noreen," Berta and I hit the road. We started in Los Angeles and headed east. Winter was setting in and the colder it got, the worse Noreen worked. Apparently the cold was separating the chemicals. On the day after Thanksgiving, we pulled into the leading beauty salon in Lincoln, Nebraska. It was wall-to-wall customers because Nebraska was playing Oklahoma in the big football game on Saturday. The owner of the shop was working on the wife of the president of the University of Nebraska, trying to tone the yellow out of her graying hair. A perfect situation for "Noreen."

"I have just the thing," I declared, producing the container and reeling off the virtues of the magic new rinse as I mixed it in a bowl of water. The operator applied it to the president's wife's hair and wrapped a towel around her head. Ten minutes later she unwrapped it and the poor woman's hair was a bright Kelly green.

Berta and I were out of there fast and on our way back to Seattle.

What's the tie-in to Fox's? Had the president's wife's hair turned blond instead of green, my son-in-law might be selling hair rinse right now instead of jewelry.

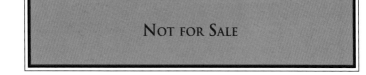

NOT FOR SALE

"I haven't bought a new car in twenty-five years," I told my son-in-law.

"At your age you don't need a new car," he replied. "You need a new driver."

That's a joke, I hope, but at 88 I'm hankering for a new car — and that new car smell — just one more time. The aroma of a new car is to men what the finest perfume is to women. Give me a tire to kick and that mesmerizing odor, and I'm ready to sign on the dotted line.

I've watched the TV ads, read the newspapers and slick magazines, and I've come to the conclusion that you don't buy a car today — you lease one! A Honda is $225 a month, a Buick, $305, a Mercedes, $575. If you write a check or pay cash, the dealer calls the IRS or the FBI. Who needs that?

So I told my son-in-law, "We should be leasing jewelry. An Omega Seamaster for $190 a month, a sapphire ring and earring set for $300 a month, or even a .76 carat,

E color, VVS Lazare Kaplan Ideal Cut diamond for $490 a month. How does that sound?"

"Sound's great," he said. "It's called 'credit.'"

Why didn't I think of that?

To get back to the car, I didn't buy one. Kicked a few tires and found out that cars talk back these days.

My son-in-law gave me some "new car" fragrance for my birthday. I sprayed it in my 1972 Mercedes. Now it smells like a 1927 Packard.

Oh, well.

SIDNEY THAL

SENSITIVITY

My son-in-law says the older I get, the more sensitive and touchy I become. (He may have said "grouchy." I'm a little hard of hearing these days.)

"Every time I say I don't like one of your ads, you pout!" he moans. "After all, no one is perfect. Hemingway wrote a few dogs. Even Michelangelo had to repaint a ceiling or two." Of course, Michelangelo was lucky enough to have Charlton Heston help him. I have to do it all myself.

Sounds logical, I guess, but I just can't get used to the notion that my little pearls of wisdom should be fooled around with. I have letters from readers in the advertising and journalism profession that have led me to believe what I do is good. In the first place they just can't believe I write the ads. One even says "Don't listen to anyone. Believe in your sixth sense, and go with it. Don't change."

So you can see, my poor son-in-law doesn't have it easy. If I'm "touchy" now, just think what I'll be like ten years from now when I'm ninety six.

38

People are not the only ones that are sensitive and need TLC. Many gems fall into that category. For instance, your pearls should not be put around your neck until your hair has been sprayed and your perfume applied (of course, my son-in-law says not to bother with hair spray and perfume in the first place). Be sure to wipe them with a silk cloth or other soft material before you put them away, and avoid getting the cord wet. Pearls may need to be restrung every few years if worn often.

Emeralds should be worn like a cashmere sweater; they are more delicate and you should take special care. So please, no rock climbing or gardening. The good news is that rubies and sapphires can be worn most of the time, as they are the hardest and most durable of all the colored gems other than fancy-colored diamonds.

Opals are fragile, and should be worn like a fine silk blouse, but are certainly worth the special care. Each one is unique. They range from soft pastels to fire opals' deep, peacock greens and reds.

So maybe if I am "sensitive," it's because of the business I'm in.

> ## HOW LONG DOES AN 84-YEAR-OLD ADVERTISING COPYWRITER HAVE?

"Like a superstar athlete, a franchise advertising copywriter's career may be short lived. Once in a millennium an advertising copywriter comes along with the rare ability to write words so powerful that they can arrest the human mind. You are advertising's answer to the bionic man. And you should be compensated accordingly."

That's just one of the many letters I have received in response to my ads for Fox's. I have hired the lawyer who wrote it to represent me in contract negotiations with my son-in-law.

My son-in-law responded to my agent: "Sid's ads are great. Hall of Fame material. I know he has to think of his family — I'm one of them — but don't you think a twenty-year contract for an 84-year-old is a bit long?

"Furthermore, I have to put customers first. You know what happens when the Mariners give Ken Griffey $26 million, or when the Sonics buy a 7-foot center, or the

Seahawks try to sign the number one draft choice? Prices go up. As it is, you can go to Canlis for the price of a hot dog and a beer at the Kingdome.

"And what's this demand for fringe benefits? I know the old London taxi's 40 years old, but I really don't think he needs a brand new English Austin Cab. I told him if business was good we'd consider one of those new robot golf carts (he says he wants to walk, but he's tired of carrying his clubs) and we'll throw in a new typewriter. But the life insurance policy is absolutely out of the question. And I think he should keep the ads coming while we resolve this matter, even if it has to go to binding arbitration."

"Hold out," my agent says. "Fox's is a great store, but he needs your advertising genius. He'll come around. Trust me."

To my son-in-law: This is not personal — business is business.

LOOK WHO'S UPSET NOW!

My son-in-law has been in such a good mood lately that I can hardly believe it. Do you think that it's because I've been south for the winter? The last thing I did before returning to Seattle was see Tracy, my young, beautiful and talented therapist. Before I could even get comfortable in a large overstuffed chair and open my mouth, she pounced.

"Sid!" she demanded. "Why are you so furious with your son-in-law?"

"I'm not," I said. "Moe and I get along very well."

"It's not Cindy's husband I'm talking about. It's Joy's, the one that runs your store in Seattle." Then she waved a bunch of my ads, her long red fingernails flashing a warning.

"Don't tell me there isn't some truth in all this cutesy stuff you've been running in *Alaska Airlines Magazine* and elsewhere. I bet all your readers can't wait for your next soap opera episode. At first I thought you had a ghost writer like Nancy Reagan or General Schwartzkopf, but this stuff is too real. You are upset, aren't you?"

"Gee whiz, Tracy," I replied in defense. "We should switch chairs. You're the one who's upset — you didn't even say hello, give me five or a hug when I came in. And I'm not going to talk to you about my son-in-law. He's doing an outstanding job, although..."

"Yes?"

"Well, he did go out and buy a 16-foot tall mastodon fossil and installed it in the store. To make room, he moved Berta and me out of our office."

"Aha! Gotcha. And how did it feel when you found out that your office was gone along with all your memorabilia. Like those letters from Presidents Reagan, Bush, and Clinton thanking you for the jade putters you'd given them. That hurt, I bet."

She cut me off before I could respond. "Don't answer because your time is nearly up. Sorry we did not have time to analyze your golf swing. See you in the fall, and next time, try to remember what you came to see me about."

"Don't worry, Tracy," I sputtered. "I only forget a few things — like paying my bill when I leave this office!"

(Fox's mastodon is now displayed at the Burke Museum on the University of Washington campus.)

To My Son-In-Law: An Editorial

As far as the contract for my future services as advertising manager is concerned, I think we should clear up something that's been bothering me. I never said you didn't look good in sweats. And just because I wear a necktie on the golf course doesn't mean you should wear a necktie in the store, but I think sweats and tennis shoes are entirely inappropriate.

The very fact that the evening jacket has been replaced by the bomber jacket on the Great White Way is the reason that you should stand up (in your dinner jacket) and be counted. Sure it's the age of comfort, but Fox's isn't Denny's.

I know I'm 84 years old and I tie my tie with a Windsor knot, but there are still bastions of proper attire left. Even in Seattle. Sometimes you need the courage to buck the trends. I know you tell me the Northwest has perfected the art of casual dressing and that our challenge as a fine jewelry store is to offer beautiful diamonds set to look wonderful all day and into the evening, watches that look great with a suit and can still go on the tennis court or sailing. Providing jewelry that appeals to the individual instead of the masses.

My friends read the national business magazines and tell me the jewelry trade isn't as good most places as it is at Fox's. They tell me I should get off your back, that you are doing even better than I did when I ran Fox's, that you must be some kind of child prodigy and I'm going to lose you to Starbucks or Spot Bagel. They say as long as people are happy they should wear anything they want and I should be quiet.

Maybe they're right. But when I was president of Fox's I dressed like the Chancellor of the Exchequer. Wherever did you get the idea that tennis shoes with different colored laces are fashionable? We don't agree on everything, but I still love you. Keep up the good work.

P.S. How are you getting along with my contract? (I see you finally got a haircut.)

A REBUTTAL

S ummer may have been too short for you, but it was a long time for me. My father-in-law usually flies south when the weather gets cold. Last year he left on September 9th. This year he said he wasn't leaving until the rainy season set in.

It was a dry fall. We did a rain dance, but it didn't work.

Don't get me wrong, I love my father-in-law. He's the greatest teacher in the history of the jewelry business. He taught me everything I know, and I am indebted to him. I know this because he reminds me of it constantly.

But the truth is he drives me crazy about our advertising. He really wants me to return to those old TV commercials showing him driving his English cab up Fifth Avenue, wearing his bowler, and peering back through the door looking for customers.

I say those ads are old hat. They send the wrong message. People think you have to be old, rich, and take a limousine to shop here.

We could photograph our jewelry, but those ads pretty much look the same. I want to show people the real thing — gold, platinum, and beautiful natural gem stones. I want them to feel the difference when they pick up a hand-made chain or a real gold watch.

I admit I'd rather spend money on great merchandise than on advertising. I prefer buying a wonderful emerald or great designer piece for the store to spending thousands of dollars on an ad in the Sunday paper or on a 30-second TV spot that you might miss when you switch channels.

We have to keep our costs down to keep our prices competitive. When our customers tell us how, locally and nationally, we have the finest merchandise at the best price, we know we're doing our job.

I also know that people enjoy reading Sid's ads, but customers don't necessarily relish paying for them. That's why you don't get to read as many as you might like.

But we can assure customers that they won't be disappointed when they come to Fox's. That's my goal, that's my job.

Chai Mann

P.S. To my father-in-law: This isn't personal — business is business.

LIFE AND LOVE:

WHAT'S IN A NAME?

Harry Fox started Fox's in 1912 at the corner of 2nd and Union. When Berta and I bought Fox's on January 9, 1948, we didn't have the money to put our name on the windows. Besides that, the store came with reams of new stationery.

Poor we were, but not dumb, so Fox's stayed Fox's. Other people have different ideas about their names.

Cindy, my daughter the writer, recently told me she had changed the spelling of her name to "Cyndy." That's okay — just so she doesn't change her last name.

My youngest daughter, Pamela, went to the University of California twenty-five years ago. Her friends said she was no Pamela, and influenced her to change her name to Joy.

I asked my friend J. Kelly Farris, Ph.D., what the J. stood for. He said, "Jamie. Can you imagine a big Irishman like me going through Marine boot camp with a first name like Jamie?"

Unlike a lot of immigrants, my father got through Ellis

Island with his family name intact. When he arrived in Boston, however, friends and relatives told him he should change it.

"What kind of a name is Thal?"

"In German it means 'Valley,'" he explained.

"German, shmerman," they argued. "It's too short and it's too harsh. Why not make it beautiful, like Blumenthal or Rosenthal?"

So Father took out his citizenship papers in the name of Rosenthal in 1906. It worked out well enough until he came to Bellingham where his four brothers had lived since the turn of the century. Now here comes another brother named Rosenthal. After seven years of confusion, he went to court to change it back legally to what it had been in the first place!

If you are bewildered by all this, imagine my poor piano teacher. She loved my name, "Sidney Rosenthal." At fourteen, my Chopin recital was standing room only. The most famous concert pianist of the twenties was Moritz Rosenthal. With a name like his, I was a real drawing card, but Thal? Well, I haven't given any recitals lately.

What's in a name? Change it if you so desire! It could be like chicken soup — it can't hurt you — but I like to think that Harry Fox would have been proud of us for not tinkering with his.

GROWING OLD

Professional people are hired to improve your life. Most important in this group is the doctor. When I have an appointment, I imagine him talking to himself...

My Doctor:

It's that Sid again. The man is 88 years old! The way he is going, he will probably outlive me. I'm working my butt off to send my kids to college and buy that beautiful ring at Fox's for my wife's 50th birthday, and he's complaining about getting out of breath after 18 holes of golf in the 100 degree heat. His hip replacement was done 25 years ago and his pacemaker is as old as some of my unpaid accounts.

My Attorney:

What's Sid up to now!? Probably wants to change his will again. Maybe he parked his London cab in a fire lane and thinks he can get away with it. Or did he get a ticket for speeding? I told him not to use Hertz in that ad without their permission.

My Banker:

I bet Sid has screwed up his checking account. The last time was the worst. He wrote nine checks on a closed account — checks bounced like Sampra's 125 mile-per-hour serve. He insists it was our fault. The account was closed three years ago. Doesn't he throw anything away?

My Accountant:

Why doesn't he let my office handle everything — pay his bills, do his check book, take care of his tax returns? Life could be so simple. He is getting forgetful, missed his car insurance payment and failed to renew his driver's license. Yet he never misses an appointment for lunch or golf.

My Insurance Broker:

At 88, Sid's insurance policies were paid up years ago! Wonder what he wants now? The last time I talked to him, he threw me out of his office. The life insurance policy he was interested in was nearly 100 percent premium. What's the life expectancy at 88? Would you believe 93?

My Golf Pro:

Here he is again, still taking lessons. At 88 he wants to hit the ball like Tiger Woods (he says he'll settle for Fred Couples). I hate taking his money, sort of....

My Tailor:

Can you believe that Sidney? Ordered a suit with two pairs of pants.

My Grocer:

The man's a real optimist — he still buys green bananas.

BERTA THAL
1911-1996

Fly away my dearest one
Fly away into the sky
The time has come
Leave your body here
It supports you not
Arise
Like the butterfly
Fly away into the sun

I wrote this poem for Berta a few weeks before she died on April 23, 1996.

This beautiful lady touched everyone she met. Berta was a fighter. Her standards were high. Only perfection was tolerated. Friend or foe were taken to task if they didn't do their very best.

You went through a tough interview when you applied for a job at Fox's.

"Why do you want to work at Fox's?" she'd ask. If she didn't hear or feel the following answers — "Fox's is the best store in the city, I am qualified, I am punctual, I am honest" — your chances of being hired were about as good as those of the proverbial snowball in Hades.

Berta was my partner — my wife, my life — and together we went from a Mom-and-Pop-store in 1948 to today's beautiful shop at Fifth & Union in downtown Seattle.

Berta set the example for all fine jewelers with her style and integrity, and her love of the profession.

Life goes on...

I will miss her.

BLIND DATE

I haven't been on a blind date for seventy years! In 1926, my high school doubles partner invited me to take his sister to our senior prom. It was a disaster!

Before she passed on, my wife Berta warned me, "Beware of women bearing casseroles." She was one smart lady.

After 62 years of marriage, it's lonely no matter how busy you are. What swinging I do these days is with my favorite Callaway driver. At my age, any date — blind or otherwise — is pretty frightening.

And things have changed in seventy years. Some women hardly tarry a decent interval.

"You know, Sidney," says one. "I have this friend who has a beautiful home and swimming pool right on a fabulous golf course. She is younger than you [who isn't?] and she wants to meet you. She's a great cook and loves to go skinny dipping."

Skinny dipping? Lonely I am, but not that lonely!

PRESS # FOR MORE INFORMATION

I've had it with the telephones, I've had it with "Please hold." By the time they get back to me, I've forgotten why I called. I've had it with "Please press one for the next menu." I don't need a menu, I just had lunch.

Just last week I flew to Chicago. While waiting at the airport, I was called to the White Courtesy Telephone. It took me ten minutes to find the phone and when I dialed the number, I got the response: "Press 1 for menu, 2 for parking garage, 3 for Hertz, 4 for Alamo, 5 for Yellow Cab, 6 for...." By that time I was frantic and dialed "O" for operator, and found myself back in the menu again. After five minutes I gave up. My plane was just about to leave and I never did find out who was trying to reach me.

I called my doctor the other day and after that voice said "Please Hold," this is what I got: "Please enter your name, your social security number, and press pound." What is "pound" and where the heck is it? When I pressed "#" I felt like I was going to get in trouble and would soon need an attorney. "We cannot recognize your code," the machine responded. "Please press star to get out of cycle and dial again. Thank you."

Thank God it wasn't critical when I called the doctor. I was going to invite him to a golf game. In the old days, all I had to do was call his nurse and mention golf and he would drop his scalpel and get on the line. If I really needed to see a doctor at age 87 and had to go through this baloney four or five times, I'd just die of aggravation.

A DREAM

Madeline opened the door and welcomed me into her office. She is my favorite therapist at the Hospice and a former nun with a doctorate in psychology.

"Let's see," she said as I sat down. "Your Berta has been gone six months now. How are you getting along?"

"OK, I guess. I get a little upset about a few things."

"Tell me about it. We have plenty of time."

"Well, my children removed everything that might remind me of Berta as soon as she was buried. Took down her portrait and all the photos, removed her clothes, jewelry, furs, even her soap and perfume. Everything's gone except her hearing aid."

"Did that make you angry?"

"Not really. They can't take her out of my mind, but that's my problem."

"What do you mean?"

"I can only see her as she was in the last three years of

her illness. I can't recall how she looked the other sixty years of our marriage."

"You can't remember anything about her from before?"

"I can't picture her at all. How she looked when we went to high school, in college, how beautiful she was at our wedding. Now that all the photos are gone, I can't refresh my memory and I don't even dream about her. All that's left is her hearing aid."

"You keep coming back to that hearing aid. Why?"

"Because, Madeline, she got it just before she died. It's the best money can buy. Now I need a hearing aid, and my doctor says he can adapt Berta's for me."

"A hearing aid is a very personal thing. I'm not sure it's the right thing to do, unless it's an issue of money."

"Well, they are expensive and it takes months to get a new one."

Madeline considered this. "Why don't you just try it for a few weeks and then we'll talk about it again. Meanwhile, don't worry about your memories of Berta. People often can't remember a loved one's face after a tragedy, but they come back."

I had the hearing aid adapted to my ear, but I hesitated before using it. One night I had this dream.

I was wearing the aid and driving my car alone. Suddenly Berta was yelling in my ear.

"Don't go so fast! Watch out for that crazy driver! Stop for God's sake!"

Then I was at a dinner party and flirting with various

women. Berta was in my ear again, "Not that one, she's too fat. No, she's too thin. Not her, too young. And that one's too old."

An old friend came up to talk. "Not with her, you don't," Berta hissed in my ear. "I always hated her."

Still in my dream, I left the party and went home to bed. Then I head Berta's voice chiding me.

"When you go to the bathroom, don't forget to put the toilet seat down after you're done!"

I woke up in a sweat, turned on the light and looked at the hearing aid, which was sitting in a velvet box on the bedside table. I closed the lid and never opened it again.

My hearing is a lot better now — and so are my memories of Berta. But what do I tell Madeline when I see her?

THREE HOLES-IN-ONE... OR WAS IT FOUR?

The older I get the better I was. It's like a fish story: the four-inch minnow becomes a twenty-pound salmon. I don't think I'm that bad an exaggerator, but I do find my mediocre exploits becoming more and more grandiose.

For instance, I was a good tennis player as a young man. City champion of Bellingham in 1927 (says so on my trophy), but to hear me tell of my exploits, you'd think I was Bill Tilden or Poncho Gonzales. I did play two sets with the great Elly Vines. He was junior champion and I won four games (maybe it was only two).

In golf, I was never better than a twenty handicap, although I've had three holes-in-one. This part is absolutely 100 percent true, so help me.

Berta bought a seven wood for my 65th birthday. I hit it only once and retired it on the second hole at Glendale, par 3, 130 yards. The photo and story made Golf Digest. When I tell about the distance it gets longer and longer. Now it's 175 yards.

Have I told you about my operations, my heart attack, my stroke, my hip replacement? At 88, most of the doctors who gave me a lifetime guarantee have passed on. The great Dr. Ernie Burgess did one of his first hip replacements on me. I think I was his favorite patient. He would call me to come into his office and have me perform a crab walk on my hands and knees, to demonstrate to a reluctant patient how successful that operation could be.

I've had the same hip for 25 years, but why is it so much more fun to say "thirty years" and that I'm the oldest living recipient with an original hip replacement?

If you think I overdo it when it comes to Fox's, you should come in and judge for yourself. I think Fox's gets better as I get older, and that's no baloney.

What You Smell Is What You Get

Took the wrapping off *Town & Country* magazine. Could hardly wait to see all the beautiful ads between its slick covers. Then it hit me in the nose. Remember when it used to be "What you see is what you get?" Well, I've got news for you. It's not that way anymore! The newest gimmick in slick magazine advertising is "What you smell is what you get." I should have been on my guard because there was a slight aroma before I picked up the magazine, but I was too anxious to see what was new in merchandising.

I opened page three and there was *Discover Safari*. In an instant my allergies discovered that this expedition was not the one for me. The scent was overwhelming and I rushed to turn the page only to find *Tuscany — It Draws Fire to the Moon!*

More like Draws Fire to My Eyes! — please pass the tissues. By this time I was gasping for breath and my son-in-law had to call 911. Next thing I knew, I was in the emergency ward. The doctor gave me some pills and said "Sid, maybe you need a dog with a good nose to warn you of an overdose of magazine fragrance. That's a joke, ha, ha."

The worst part is I love perfume. It's wonderful in its place, but what comes bursting out from a magazine is another matter. After a few days in recovery, I decided the doctor's advice wasn't so silly and went to a pet shop.

They told me about a Great Dane with the "Best Nose In The Business," but he wasn't for sale yet. His owner ran a perfumery in Tacoma. It seems that when she was at work, all was well, but when she got home, the dog would go crazy from the odors on her clothes. He would bark and growl and try to bite her. Now she has to decide whether to sell the dog or get out of the business.

I had hoped to make her an offer for that dog that she couldn't refuse, but my son-in-law vetoed it. You see, we have a 16-foot-tall mastodon in Fox's, who is 12,000 years old and a museum piece. He doesn't smell, but, well, what self-respecting dog could resist a pile of bones like that?

ANOTHER BLIND DATE

My family and friends mean well. They know I'm lonely without Berta after 62 years of marriage, and insist on "fixing me up"!

I really don't need "fixing up." I've got professionals for that (don't get too far ahead of me!!!): my orthopedic surgeon fixed me up with a hip replacement and my cardiologist fixed me up with a pacemaker. With the lawyers, accountants, mechanics I'm, "fixed up" for life.

I tell my friends, "I'm okay, just let me be," but they still insist on fixing me up.

So here we go with another blind date. Except this one wasn't totally sight-unseen. I'd met this gal at the U of W in 1930, and remembered her as a cute blonde, thin freshman. My friends arranged for me to take her to dinner at Canlis.

Things change in sixty years. She's no longer cute, or blonde, or thin and she's no freshman — she really knows her way around. The lady was upset with me because I drove too slow, ate too fast, and turned on the radio to listen to the Mariners. She'll probably never call me back again and I don't blame her. I've changed, too, and I'm no bargain either.

After years as a caregiver, I really am enjoying my privacy and freedom. When my friends aren't trying to "fix" this, total strangers take a hand.

The other day I was shopping in QFC when I noticed this lady following me around. She pointed out the tomatoes I should buy and then shook her head when I picked up a T-Bone steak and steered me toward the skinless chicken breasts.

"Do I know you?" I asked as we approached the checkout counter.

"I don't think so," she replied, smiling. "You remind me of my third husband."

"How nice, I guess. How many times have you been married?" I asked.

"Twice."

GROWING OLDER

A funny thing happened to me on the way to the golf course a few years ago: I had a stroke. Boy was I scared! Not really, but it sounds good and makes great copy. Larry King was scared to death when he had a heart attack and even wrote a book about it.

I was playing on the O'Donnell's golf course in Palm Springs. I had this terrible pain low in my stomach as I hit my ball over the mountain on number 5, except it didn't go over the mountain. I didn't know if that caused the pain, so I went to the doctor's office.

While I was waiting for the doctor to see me, I felt the little snap in my head and started losing my speech. It was like it was happening to someone else. I was over to one side, watching what was going on with some amazement, as the numbness tingled down my right side.

My speech came back quickly and then the feeling in my right arm. I laughed and said, "I'm okay, let's go home." Then I realized I had no feeling in my fingers.

The doctor finally came in and said, "Shoot, get him into the hospital." I didn't get to my room and on a blood thinner until much later. But this isn't a tale about hospitals, doctors, cat scans, echo grams, and God knows what else. No, it's about the positive attitude and laughter that make you well.

I knew right away that I had to get the feeling back in the three fingers of my right hand that remained paralyzed — need them for golf and writing. I started telling my brain to get going and help me with my rehab.

My daughter, Cindy, picked me up from Desert Hospital five days after the stroke. I asked her to drive by O'Donnell's. When we got there, she asked, "Okay, now what?"

"You can drive me home now," I explained. "I just wanted to see if the flag was at half-mast for me!"

I hit 20 balls the week after the stroke. The doctor said it was okay if I just used an 8 iron. I did end up playing one hole with some guys. I hit two 8-iron shots and sunk the putt for a par!

It made me stop and think about why I, an 86-year-old man with a hip replacement (that's worn out and needs replacing), a pacemaker (that probably needs a new battery), and now a stroke, was somehow singled out to stick around.

Somehow I don't think God spared me just to golf. So why?

Every day I'm working hard to find the answer.

SHORT FICTION

The Violin
The Fire
The Rabbi
The Dancers

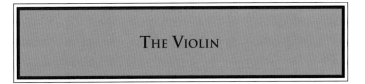

THE VIOLIN

The only thing he saw in the window of the new store that opened in Bellingham's "Old Town" was the violin. There were many other items on display, but the violin was like a beacon in a lighthouse. The fine, red-polished wood glowed, beckoned him to hold it under his chin, cradle it to his bosom. And there, beside the fiddle was the horsehair bow.

As if by command and with a swish of a baton, his mind opened and memories poured out. Thoughts held back for nearly ten years: the cold, the snow, muddied roads, gypsy camps, and the violins.

Suddenly, the year was 1909 and he was five years old, living in Spokishok, a small Lithuanian shtetl. The Czar and the Russian bear were on the prowl. They overran and gobbled up their neighbors.

Soon, his father would leave for a new life in America, later to send for the family, but first they had to survive the cold winter. Their homes were only thatched huts with dirt floors, and the livestock were moved indoors to share their body heat.

The gypsies, who were camped on the edge of town, had it worse. They lived in their wagons or in tents, always on the move. His father brought them potatoes and fresh, hot black bread that his mother had baked early in the morning. This was a gift to the chieftain of the gypsies and an invitation for him to trade their wares for food.

As he and his father approached the encampment with the provisions, the sound of the violins called to him. The resonant vibrations and singing of the strings invaded his mind. The melody of the song surrounded his heart. He found it hard to breathe.

Where were the musicians? He and his father rounded the bend and there, on a small platform, the music flowed out from a gray curly-headed man, a tall dark lad with a moustache, and a blond girl with a child-size violin.

On and on they played. One melody after another. Hungarian, Russian, old tunes, new tunes, with passion and tenderness the music soared. The little child somehow kept up with the others, her bow in perpetual motion.

Tears came to the boy's eyes. "Papa," he cried. "What music the fiddle makes! It's so beautiful. Can I have a violin like the little girl's?"

"Someday, my child, someday," his father responded.

"Papa, I've got to have a violin. I've got to make music."

"God willing," his father replied

That was ten years ago. Ten hard, painful years.

The jingle of the bell as the door of the store opened brought him back to the reality of the present. Heart thumping, he went to the counter and approached the clean-shaven, elderly clerk. He did not trust his voice because it was changing. Finally, swallowing hard, he squeaked out, "How much is the violin?"

"Twelve dollars with bow and case. I've seen you looking at it before. Here's the case. It's lined in velvet."

"I haven't got twelve dollars. I've got a dollar and four bits."

"Well, guess you're a few bits short, young fellow."

The boy turned to go, but stopped. "Can I see the violin, please?"

The storekeeper went to the window and slid the glass open. He took out the violin and put it in the boy's hands. They shook as he held the beautiful instrument. As he stroked the strings, the sound startled him. Gently, instinctively, his fingers touched the pegs to tune it.

"Thank you," he said, returning the fiddle. "I'll come back when I get more money saved. I'm your newsboy."

"I know," the owner said with a smile. "Tell you what I'm going to do, young fellow. This isn't an ordinary violin. This is a pawn shop, and the man who left it was a fine musician. It's been a month and I guess he isn't coming back. Give me the dollar and a half and I'll put the violin away for you. When you get twelve dollars paid, it's yours."

And that's how the violin became his. It was the one he took his first lessons on from Madame Engberg, and then from Professor Vaughn Arthur, who came weekends from Seattle. The one he took to the Juilliard School in New York. The one he taught with for more than sixty years -- his first and only violin.

THE FIRE

I hurried down Holly Street towards my father's store, which was located on the edge of the city's "Old Town." Papa had told me to come straight from school, and I'd wondered why all day.

He was out front, pacing impatiently. He put his arm around my shoulders and drew me into the store.

"What's going on, Papa?"

He licked his lips, swallowed hard, and whispered, "I'm going to burn down the store."

"What?" I jumped as if he had shouted the words. "What did you say?"

"Shh! This has to be a secret between you and me. I said I'm going to burn down the store."

"That's crazy! You don't mean it." I couldn't understand this kind of talk from him. "Why do you want to do such a thing?"

"I need the insurance money to pay the bills, to send you to college. You know what's happening with outfits like Sears and Penney's coming to town. My little store's going to go down the drain."

I stared at my father as if he were a stranger. "Papa, don't do it. You'll go to jail for arson, maybe murder. Don't forget Madam Jones and her girls living upstairs. They could burn to death."

"No they won't. The walls and stairs have asbestos. It doesn't burn. I've thought it all out," he added, pulling down the shade that read "Store Closed."

Papa nudged me toward the fireplace, where a ladder leaned against the mantel. He climbed halfway up and pressed a small button that I'd never noticed before. A secret panel slid open, revealing a metal money box. I craned my neck and saw a fat, white candle standing on a shelf. It was surrounded by a coil of oiled rope and a pile of birch chips.

"See," he explained, "the candle will burn down to the rope and start a fire with lots of smoke. Everyone will have plenty of warning to get out. I went down to the creek and tried it out. It'll work, I tell you."

"But Papa, what if the girls are drunk and don't wake up." I pointed to the heavily oiled wood flooring. "The whole building will go up in a flash. You're creating a death trap. Please forget it. Find the money another way, run a sale, go to the bank and get a loan."

"I already ran a sale, and Mr. Gillespie at the bank said no more loans. No, this is the only way."

"Then just go bankrupt," I pleaded.

"I would never do that," Papa exclaimed. "Being bankrupt is a terrible thing. How would it look for me and my family! Even Mama's people back in Boston would hear about it."

"My God, Papa, I think going to jail for arson or maybe murder is a lot worse. And you hate violence. You can't even cut off the head of a chicken for supper. If you don't stop this crazy talk, I'm going to tell Mama."

Papa stared at me for a long time. Then he sighed, closed the alcove and climbed back down the ladder with tears in his eyes.

"You're right, my son, you're right. What was I thinking? Forget I ever talked to you, I'm just an old fool."

I tried to do as Papa said, but everytime I heard fire engines, I couldn't help thinking of that hidden candle, the rope, and the girls living above the store.

A few months later, I was awakened at 5 o'clock on a Sunday morning by clanging alarm bells. I had papers to deliver anyway, so I dressed and looked outside. I saw smoke coming from the direction of the store.

"Papa!" I shouted, "there's a fire in Old Town!"

He threw on some clothes and we ran side by side to the store. Sure enough, flames and thick smoke were erupting from its windows and the rooms above. There was no sign of Madam Jones and her girls.

"Oh God, please let them be safe," I prayed to myself, thinking the worse. When I turned away, I found my plea answered: Madam Jones and her scantily clad entourage stood across the street with Mr. Gillespie, the banker who also happened to own the building.

While the girls watched the firemen trying to douse the flames, Jones and Gillespie laughed as if sharing a private joke. Papa and I crossed the street to talk to them.

"It's all my fault," cried Betty, Madam Jones's live-in maid. "If I hadn't gone to care for my sick brother, this wouldn't have happened."

"There, there, dearie, don't go blamin' yourself," Madam Jones said. "It's not your fault one of the girls fell asleep with a cigarette. I warned them to be more careful, but they don't listen to me. Anyway, we'll be back in business very soon," she added with a wink at the banker.

"Move it, kid," commanded a reporter from the local paper as he shoved me aside. He was joined by our insurance man, and they both began questioning my father and the rest of the group.

The next day's newspaper reported that the fire had been caused by a careless smoker, and Papa and everyone else received generous insurance settlements. I kept my own suspicions to myself for thirty long years. Then my father fell ill and I was summoned to his sickbed.

"It's time I told you the truth about that fire," he began, with a mischievous grin. "Most everyone's gone, so it can't hurt anybody...."

"Papa, I don't need to know," I interrupted.

"It's not what you think. I didn't burn down the store — Madam Jones did."

"Why would she do that?"

"Gillespie was building a new hotel. He wanted her to come in as a partner, but she didn't have enough money. When her maid took the night off, she put a wide candle in her room and let it burn down to the floor. She waited until the planks caught fire and then she got the girls out."

"Papa, are you sure you're not making this up?"

"It's the truth," he declared, with a smile on his face. "So help me God!"

Papa died soon after. I never thought to ask him where Madam Jones got that candle.

THE RABBI

"The new rabbi is coming to town!"

The news spread among Bellingham's thirty Jewish families like the call of Paul Revere. Everyone was excited, my parents, the older congregants, even the small children.

We bar mitzvah boys were more thrilled than anyone else when we learned that the new rabbi had played baseball in college, at Notre Dame of all places. Our group wanted more than anything to play in the church league, but we needed a coach and trainer. Now one would arrive on the Sunday train.

That day at the railroad station, you would have thought the Barnum and Bailey Circus was coming to town on the High Holidays. Scrubbed, dressed in our best clothes, impatient, we boys couldn't stand waiting on the platform. When we heard the engine roar around the bend, its bell clanging and brakes screeching, we charged down the tracks to greet the train from Vancouver, British Columbia.

The young rabbi jumped from the moving coach as if he were Douglas Fairbanks doing a stunt in a movie. He resembled Fairbanks in other ways: tall and thin, but wearing a trimmed blue-black beard. His black circular hat fell from his curly hair when he landed on the platform. I picked it up and handed it to him, noticing his bright blue eyes. "Thank you, boychick," he said and carefully replaced the hat to leave his earlocks showing. He patted my shoulder and added, "That was kind of you."

My Uncle Louie was chairman of the board of the Congregation Beth Am. He took the rabbi by the arm and introduced him to the welcoming crowd. Then he drove the rabbi to the farm of Jake and Sarah, where he was to stay temporarily.

Finding a home for the rabbi had not been easy. I knew this from working after school in Louie's secondhand store. He held the congregation board meetings in his back room every other Friday, and I overheard the debate when word arrived that the rabbi would come west from New York without his wife for a trial period in Bellingham.

"Who's the rabbi going to stay with?" Uncle Louie asked. He ruled himself out because his house was already filled with a wife and four sons.

Hyman explained that he had four daughters.

Joseph had just gotten married and had no desire to take in a boarder.

Jacob was moving to Seattle soon.

So the Board nominated Jake and Sarah. They had a

small farm north of town and their children were grown. They could use the extra money.

Sarah kept a spotless Kosher home and was regarded as the best cook in town. She baked bread, cookies, bagels, and challah for Friday nights, and also sold fresh milk, butter, sour cream, and a delicious cottage cheese with chives. Despite her forty-plus years of hard work, she was tall and graceful and her blond hair showed only a few streaks of gray.

Her husband never accompanied her to the synagogue, not even on Yom Kippur. Jake was not a religious man, but he worked hard raising cows and chickens and growing potatoes, squash and corn. He had no objection to hosting the rabbi, especially when Uncle Louie offered Sarah $25 for the first month's room and board.

It was a generous sum, and some of the women kvetched that it was too much. "Please, God," Uncle Louie prayed aloud, "let me finish my term as chairman in peace, alive if possible, and without committing murder."

The congregation pitched in and remodeled the small house of worship for the new rabbi, and he took to his duties with vigor. He had a fine tenor voice and the Friday night services were full of music and song. He also lectured at the nearby teacher's college, spoke at the Chamber of Commerce and Elks Club, organized a glee club, and best of all, started a baseball team so we older boys could finally compete in the church league.

After only a month, the board voted the rabbi a raise.

After a few more months, it offered him a three-year contract and urged him to bring his wife west and settle in Bellingham permanently.

The rabbi accepted the contract, but said his wife's father, a famous rabbi from Poland, didn't want his daughter to live so far from New York City. The board insisted that he return to collect his wife, and gave him a month's vacation in July for the trip. The rabbi left only after they made it an ultimatum: no wife, no job.

Uncle Louie was happy for the respite and counted the days to the end of his term. The store was busy with a new consignment of furniture. I was polishing a diningroom table in the shop one afternoon when the phone rang. It was the circulation manager of the *Bellingham Herald* calling for my uncle. I could hear his voice crackling from the handset.

"Louie, I've got this crazy letter from your rabbi. We billed him two dollars for his newspapers, but there's no check enclosed. Just some strange kind of writing."

Uncle Louie sent me to pick up the letter. I sneaked a look inside the envelope, saw that the letter was written in Yiddish, and raced back to the store.

Uncle Louie's face turned ashen as he turned the pages of the rabbi's letter. At the end, he yelled out a Russian a curse, "Yah Bitveryamat!" He had served six years in the Russian army and it was the worst swear word he ever uttered.

He then summoned the board to an emergency meeting at the store. I retired unnoticed to a corner while they gathered around the table I had been polishing and listened as my uncle translated the rabbi's letter aloud:

"My Dear Sarah — It is only a week since I left your embrace and the comfort of your sweet bosom. I do not know how long I can live without you. Try as I will and know I should, my mind is constantly aflame with you — your lips, your hands, your body. I can hardly breathe.

"My poor wife weeps as I turn away from her. 'What have I done,' she asks. 'Please turn to me so I can hold and kiss you. My dearest, what has become of our love?'

"How can I tell her what has happened to me? What can I do? Where can I go? What is to become of me? Surely God has foresaken me...."

Uncle Louie took off his glasses and let out a sigh. "There are two more pages of the same, except more descriptive."

The board members nodded as if to say "Enough already!" but no one spoke. Then Uncle Louie announced that he had summoned Jake to join them.

Jake tramped in a few minutes later, dressed in a yellow slicker, black coveralls, and rubber boots to the knee. Tall and gaunt, he looked more like the captain of a Puget Sound tug boat than a farmer, and he fixed the group with stern, defiant eyes.

He refused the offer of a chair and stood silently while Uncle Louie read the letter aloud. Jake put up his hand before Uncle was half way through the epistle.

"So you've had enough," Uncle Louie growled. "What do you think of your wife Sarah now? She's a curva, a whore! You should kick her out of your house."

Jake glared back. "Don't call my wife a whore, Louie, or I'll beat the hell out of you. All I know is that we've been married twenty-five years and I love her. If she's good enough for the rabbi, she's good enough for me."

And that was that. The rabbi never returned, of course, and Jake and Sarah went on living together and working their farm. I do not know if they even discussed the incident, but I've always wondered what went through Sarah's mind that day when she tore open the envelope from her beloved rabbi only to find a check for two dollars made out to the *Bellingham Herald*.

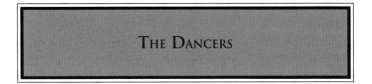

THE DANCERS

I sat alone at our table as the Lady in Black passed and whispered, "Dance with me."

Of course, I had noticed her. No one could miss her or her escort. They were spectacular dancers. He was tall, graceful, and dressed in formal white. She, too, was tall. Her hair was black as coal and swept up into a chignon. Her jet black lace gown and ebony doeskin gloves to the elbow looked heavy in the heat of the Palm Springs night.

Her face was theatrical yet somehow familiar. Or was it just the heavy make-up? Her black piercing eyes were fringed by lashes thick with mascara, and raven-colored eyebrows arched as if asking a question. And then there was the large, brilliant, pear-shaped white diamond that shimmered from the thinnest platinum chain as it nestled in the cleavage of her bosom.

There were many in the crowd who knew all about make-up and make-believe. This was the season's big media event benefiting Eisenhower Hospital. The theme, "London Town," was sponsored by the British Tourism

Agency. Mixed among the old and new movie and television greats were two former Presidents of the United States and the Duke and Duchess of Kent.

The ballroom of the Rancho Mirage Westin Hotel was decorated to look like 19th century London. Darkened backdrops depicted scenes of Trafalgar Square, the Thames, and shadowy streets along the docks. They created a somewhat sinister setting for the carefree revelers.

The south end of the ballroom disappeared into a wispy bank of artificial fog and mist. Dancers would vanish into the eerie haze, to reappear later on the north side where a champagne fountain spewed golden liquid into fluted glasses. Those who made this journey returned to their tables to tell tales of their adventures and listen to Les Brown and his Band of Renown.

I was pleased that the Lady in Black had asked me to dance with her, but I wondered why. I had not been on the floor, and had no intention of dancing with her or anyone else.

Many couples had formed a circle to watch her and her partner as they danced in the center of the room. They moved in perfect rhythm, first in the Viennese Waltz, with its quick turns and faster tempo than the traditional waltz. You knew immediately they were very good, and you waited for the band to begin the next routine of dance numbers so you could see how good they really were. In the Cha Cha, a fast Cuban dance with three basic steps and a shuffle, they became animated, and in the Rumba, the most romantic of all the Cuban dances, they doubled the beat and showed their great technique to best advantage.

But the Lady in Black seemed to be restrained in some of the Latin numbers. She postured and strutted, but was somehow not able to let herself go. What was she afraid of? What would she be like in the Paso Doble, the Spanish dance of the bull fights, with its stomping and Ole! Ole! Or the Tango, the dance of the Argentines. There should be no thin smile on her face then.

No one smiles doing the Tango. It is an aggressive, hostile encounter, a battle of the sexes. The head snaps back and forth, steps are bold, dips daring. It is controlled, but full of passion and desire. Heated bodies undulate. There's a toss away, and then they come close together again, finally spent and damp with sweat.

How long ago was it that my wife and I had been in Buenos Aires? Forty years? It was January, the height of the southern summer, and the city was sweltering and humid. Everyone who could escape was at Mar del Plata on the Atlantic where the cool breezes were a blessing. We had stayed at the newest hotel with a night club on the roof opened to the stars above.

At midnight, the dancing started in earnest. Delirious partners danced the Tango continually, never stopping. European and native, side by side. We changed partners and I was dancing with a beautiful, dark-haired Argentine girl who spun away from my grasp, impatient with my lead. She continued to center stage, and the whole room cried, "Gina! Gina!" stomping and hand clapping, cheering her on. She was hypnotic, uncontrollable, wild. The more enthusiastically the crowd responded, the more frenzied she became, until finally she fell to the floor, exhausted.

All these years later the vision of her primal, frantic dance still vibrated in my mind. The band had stopped for a short break. Our guests had left the table for the restrooms taking my wife with them, and I was alone with a warm martini.

As I got up to head for the bar, the Lady in Black passed my table and whispered again, "Dance with me." She disappeared, leaving the scent of Shalimar and memories I thought were long forgotten.

The bar was crowded and it was ten minutes before I got back to our still vacant table with a large double martini. The band started to play a new set of dances, starting with the waltz. Before I could bring the drink to my lips, I could smell the Shalimar and hear the voice. This time it commanded, "Dance with me!"

I got up from the table as if in a trance, took her arm, and led her to the floor. She was easy to dance with. Any slight pressure from my left hand, a body movement, a thought, and we were together as one. With a change to the Rumba. she came alive. There was no gentle lead now. Her movements were aggressive. I tried to rein her into my romantic style and grabbed her firmly. We compromised and went into a routine, smoothly, like ice skaters.

But it did not last. She was too restless and led us to the center of the floor where a crowd of dancers encircled us. As we passed the bandstand, she raised a gloved finger in a signal and the band began a Tango.

She was liberated. This was her dance. It consumed her, body and soul. We moved away from the other dancers toward the south concourse, dancing with a fury. Her arrogant struts and flashes of passion said, "I want you, I need you, I will take you."

Then it no longer was a dance — it was a battle. Our heads snapped in unison, our limbs ratcheted in staccato movements like robots, dramatic yet mechanical. Resentment flowed from her, charging the air between us.

Why, I wondered. Who is she and what is going on?!

Now her unspoken thoughts seemed to shout, "I could kill you!" Was it plain and simple anger, or was it something else? That she had planned this performance, I had no doubt, but why with me?

Suddenly, we were alone, gliding into the fog at the far end of the ballroom. I motioned for us to go back to our tables and tried to lead her away from the damp haze that the ice machine was churning into air. She pulled away from me and dashed through a rear door. I followed and found her alone in the dark room, with only a single lamp illuminating a small dance floor.

Strange music, drifted from invisible speakers. Yet, the Lady in Black still danced to the rhythm of the Tango. She motioned me to join her but I was exhausted.

"Come," I said, "I'm tired. You win, let's go back. Your Tango was magnificent, it brought back memories from years ago! But, I'm too old, too out of shape now. Here, let me take you back to your friend."

She did not answer but moved now in slow motion, with sluggish, exaggerated movements. She wound down like a top losing its momentum, and a strange look came over her.

Her hair was no longer midnight black. Her lace dress, gloves, everything was fading, as if the mist was bleaching out their essence. Everything about her was turning white, except the large diamond pendant on the thin platinum chain. It had turned black as coal.

She stopped dancing. She looked so weak I was afraid she would fall. I put my arm around her to escort her from the mist to safety. As I took her hand, all I could feel were bones. She started to slip from my grasp, and I looked at her. Her face was skeletal, her once voluptuous body now shrunken.

"Help! Help! Someone help us!" I called out. No one answered. We were alone. The only sound was the hiss of the huge ice machine.

"Don't die on me," I sobbed. "Hang on, don't fall. I'll never be able to pick you up."

It took all my strength to keep her from toppling to the floor. I was starting to shake in the frigid air. My evening jacket was wet, the taste in my mouth bitter.

"God," I cried, "Help me!" I didn't even know the lady's name. What would I tell her escort, or my wife?

The ice machine went into a frenzy, spewing a thick

vapor that made it difficult to see. I hung onto her desperately, yelling over and over again, "Someday help me! For God's sake help me!" It was hopeless. We were so far from everyone, there was no one to hear us.

Now an acid smell of burning filled the room, permeating our clothes, our bodies. Or what was left of her body. For she was fading into a thin outline of what she had been before.

Feeling sick to my stomach, I tried not to look at her, but I was mesmerized, spellbound. Her body was shrinking before my eyes. When I finally glanced into her face, I saw only a skull.

There was a shriek, a chilling scream as I let go and she slipped to the floor. The ice machine exploded with a bright flash and a cloud of black smoke. When it cleared, nothing remained of the Lady in Black...

Nothing except the platinum chain and its diamond, which again glowed with fierce whiteness. Reaching down to the parquet floor, I picked up the pendant and put it into the pocket of my damp dinner jacket.

Slowly, I backed out of the room and made my way across the dance floor. It was empty because the orchestra was on a break, and no one seemed to notice me. My friends and wife had not yet returned, and my martini remained untouched by my seat.

I turned and made my way unsteadily to the men's room. The attendant gave me a warm wet towel and I washed my face as he brushed my jacket. I took a swig of mouth wash, combed my hair, fixed my tie, gave the man a tip. My composure restored, I started back to my table.

Our party was just sitting down and I arrived in time to roll my wife's wheelchair into place. I slipped the pendant around her neck.

"Darling," she said, "I was so worried. I thought I had lost it. Where did you ever find it?"

Without waiting for an answer, she continued in a wistful tone. "Isn't the music wonderful? Doesn't it remind you of old times?"

Berta and Sid Thal meet Pope John Paul II in Rome

THANK YOU...

Dear Cyndy, for putting a pen in my hand when I was 83 and for saying, "No more telling -- write it!"

Palm Springs Writers Guild critique group for your helpful comments.

Chai Mann, my son-in-law, for being a good sport when my barbs made you a target.

Dear Readers, for your kind words and letters that said, "Thank you for brightening my day."

The lady at the advertising agency who wrote, "I can't believe you write this, and if you do, don't let them change your style. Trust your instincts."

Our dear customers. Without you, there would be no Fox's, no ads, no book, and no fun.

— *Sidney Thal, April 1998*